Frank Ockenfels

R.E.M. were a Georgia-born alternative rock band best known for their hits "Losing My Religion" and "Everybody Hurts." Founding members Bill Berry, Peter Buck, Mike Mills, and Michael Stipe played their first show on April 5, 1980, at a friend's birthday party in an abandoned church in Athens, Georgia. From that point forward until 2011, when they decided to call it a day, the band released fifteen albums, toured the world, won multiple GRAMMYs, two *Billboard* Music Awards, twelve MTV Video Music Awards, and were inducted into the Rock & Roll Hall of Fame, leaving a lasting legacy of great songs that defined an era.

"Shiny Happy People"
Song written by William Thomas Berry, Peter Lawrence Buck, Michael E. Mills, and John Michael Stipe
Courtesy of Universal Tunes on behalf of Night Garden Music
Used by Permission. All Rights Reserved.

LyricPop is a children's picture book collection
by LyricVerse and Akashic Books.

lyricverse.

Published by Akashic Books
Song lyrics ©1991 William Thomas Berry, Peter Lawrence Buck,
Michael E. Mills, and John Michael Stipe
Illustrations ©2021 Paul Hoppe with ShinYeon Moon

ISBN: 978-1-61775-851-5
Library of Congress Control Number: 2022931853
First printing

Printed in China

Akashic Books
Brooklyn, New York
Instagram, Twitter, Facebook: AkashicBooks
Email: info@akashicbooks.com
Website: www.akashicbooks.com

SHINY HAPPY PEOPLE

SONG LYRICS BY R.E.M.
ILLUSTRATIONS BY PAUL HOPPE
WITH SHINYEON MOON

Shiny happy people laughing

Meet me in the crowd, people, people

Throw your love around, love me, love me

Take it into town, happy, happy

Put it in the ground
where the flowers grow

Gold and silver shine

Shiny happy people holding hands
Shiny happy people holding hands

Shiny happy people laughing

Everyone around, love them, love them

There's no time to cry, happy, happy

Put it in your heart where tomorrow shines

Gold and
silver
shine

Shiny happy people holding hands

Shiny happy people holding hands

Shiny happy people holding hands
Shiny happy people holding hands

Shiny happy people laughing

Shiny happy people holding hands

Shiny happy people holding hands
Shiny happy people holding hands
Shiny happy people laughing

Shiny happy people holding hands
Shiny happy people holding hands
People, happy people

About the Illustrators

Paul Hoppe has illustrated various children's books, including *Good Vibrations*, with song lyrics by Mike Love and Brian Wilson; *How Did Humans Go Extinct?* by Johnny Marciano; *Neymar: A Soccer Dream Come True* by Mina Javaherbin; and *The Woods*, which he also wrote. His work has appeared in publications such as the *New Yorker*, the *Wall Street Journal*, and the *New York Times*. During the summer, Hoppe teaches sequential art at the School of Visual Arts. His work has been honored by the Society of Illustrators, *Communication Arts*, and *American Illustration*, among others. Originally from Poland and raised in Germany, Hoppe works from a shared studio in the Pencil Factory in Brooklyn, and lives in Queens.

ShinYeon Moon is an illustrator, educator, and aspirational shiny happy person based in New York. She holds an MFA in Illustration as Visual Essay from the School of Visual Arts. Moon's work can be found in print and online publications as well as gallery exhibitions.

LOOK OUT FOR THESE LyricPop TITLES

The 59th Street Bridge Song (Feelin' Groovy)
SONG LYRICS BY PAUL SIMON • ILLUSTRATIONS BY KEITH HENRY BROWN

Paul Simon's anthem to New York City is the joyful basis for this live-for-the-day children's picture book, providing a perfect vehicle to teach kids to appreciate life's little gifts.

African
SONG LYRICS BY PETER TOSH • ILLUSTRATIONS BY RACHEL MOSS

A beautiful children's picture book featuring the lyrics of Peter Tosh's global classic celebrating people of African descent.

(Sittin' on) The Dock of the Bay
SONG LYRICS BY OTIS REDDING AND STEVE CROPPER • IILLUSTRATIONS BY KAITLYN SHEA O'CONNOR

Otis Redding and Steve Cropper's timeless ode to never-ending days is given fresh new life in this heartwarming picture book.

Don't Stop
SONG LYRICS BY CHRISTINE McVIE • ILLUSTRATIONS BY NUSHA ASHJAEE

Christine McVie's classic song for Fleetwood Mac about keeping one's chin up and rolling with life's punches is beautifully adapted to an uplifting children's book.

Dream Weaver
SONG LYRICS BY GARY WRIGHT • ILLUSTRATIONS BY ROB SAYEGH JR.

Gary Wright's hit song is reimagined as a fantastical picture book to delight dreamers of all ages.

Good Times Roll
SONG LYRICS BY RIC OCASEK • ILLUSTRATIONS BY ROB SAYEGH JR.

Ric Ocasek's rock and roll classic—one of the Cars' greatest hit songs—leaps off the page in this exhilarating picture book.

Good Vibrations
SONG LYRICS BY MIKE LOVE AND BRIAN WILSON • ILLUSTRATIONS BY PAUL HOPPE

Mike Love and Brian Wilson's world-famous song for the Beach Boys, gloriously illustrated by Paul Hoppe, will bring smiles to the faces of children and parents alike.

Humble and Kind
SONG LYRICS BY LORI McKENNA • IILLUSTRATIONS BY KATHERINE BLACKMORE

Award-winning songwriter Lori McKenna's iconic tune—as popularized by Tim McGraw—is the perfect basis for a picture book that celebrates family and togetherness.